ie	J
j	Or
ee	Ie
oa	Ai
or	Ee
ai	Oa

Jaiden tells lies.

Jaiden painted an oak tree
and got green paint on his top.

'Paint stains, Jaiden!' cried Dad.

Abigail did it.

But Abigail did not paint.

Jaiden had a toffee...

...or ten.

'Jaiden!' moaned Dad.

Jet did it!

But Jet is just a dog.
(a black labrador)

Jaiden spilt popcorn on Dad's rug.

Jaiden,
pick it up!

Jaiden did it!
But Abigail...